# Disney Girls

## One of Us

### Gabrielle Charbonnet

Disney
PRESS

N E W   Y O R K

Printed in the United States of America.

First Edition

1   3   5   7   9   10   8   6   4   2

The text of this book is set in 15-point Adobe Garamond.

Library of Congress Catalog Card Number: 97-80295

ISBN: 0-7868-4156-7

For more Disney Press fun, visit www.DisneyBooks.com

# Contents

# Disney Girls

# One of Us

# Chapter One

# A Strong, Capable Princess

Ariel, look out!" Paula cried.

I turned around just in time to see my kitten, Rajah, pounce on the end of Ariel's long red ponytail.

"Yeow!" Ariel winced, and I winced in sympathy. I hurried over to pluck Rajah off my friend's hair, then held him against my chest.

"No, no, Rajah," I said sternly, shaking my finger at him. He batted at it with one paw. I sighed.

"I can see he's really terrified of you." Paula giggled.

Ariel was examining the end of her ponytail. "It was my

1

fault," she said. "I'm wearing this floppy scrunchie."

"Oh, well, then, of *course* he had to attack you," said Ella. She grinned.

Still holding Rajah, I sat on the floor next to Yukiko. "Scrunchie or no scrunchie," I told my kitten, "pouncing on friends is a no-no."

Rajah scrambled away, and I looked around my room. It seemed like it was full of girls, though there were only five of us: me (my name is Jasmine), Ariel, Ella, Paula, and Yukiko. Five best friends—and for a special reason. But I'll tell you about that later.

"Okay, let's get serious," said Ariel. "School is starting in just four days. What is everyone wearing the first day?"

Paula rolled her eyes. "Since it's going to be about ninety-nine degrees outside, I'm thinking shorts and a T-shirt."

Maybe in some places the first day of school is crisp and autumnlike. But here in Orlando, Florida, the days stay in the nineties practically until October. Then they plummet down into the eighties. We're pretty used to it.

"You *always* wear shorts and a T-shirt," Ariel pointed out. "I'm going to wear my green scooter skirt and my green, blue, and yellow striped top."

"I haven't even thought about what I'm going to wear," I said. "All I can think about is fourth grade! I really hope I get Ms. Benitez. I hear she's nice."

"I just hope we're together," said Paula. "I'm keeping my fingers crossed."

Paula and I were about to start fourth grade at Orlando Elementary. Ella, Yukiko, and Ariel were all going to be in third grade. They would have the teachers we'd had last year.

"Was Ms. Timmons nice?" Ella asked, looking worried.

"Yep," I said. "She's great."

"Oh, but Mrs. Henry was so awful," groaned Paula. "She's always grumpy and gives *tons* of homework."

Yukiko's brown eyes got almost round. (She's Japanese-American, with beautiful almond-shaped eyes. So when they're almost round, it means she's really surprised or worried—or both.)

"Oh, no," she wailed. "I just know I'll get Mrs. Henry!"

Ariel nudged Paula with her foot and gave her a look.

"Uh, I mean, maybe Mrs. Henry's mellowed out over

the summer," Paula said quickly. "She probably won't be so bad, if you get her."

Yukiko still looked worried. And now Ella looked worried, too. I had to change the subject—fast.

"Hey, you know what I was thinking?" I said. "I bet Jasmine never went to school at all. She probably just had court tutors."

Was I talking about myself? No, I was not. I was talking about *Princess* Jasmine, from the movie *Aladdin*. *Aladdin* is my all-time favorite movie, and Jasmine is my all-time favorite princess. And not only because we have the same name. This may sound strange, but I just totally *feel* like Jasmine, inside. When I first saw the movie, I felt as if I were looking at myself. Everything she said, I might say. All her feelings, her moods, everything—it all felt just like *me*.

Crazy? Maybe. Magical? Definitely!

"Pocahontas never went to school, either," said Paula. Yep—you guessed it. Her favorite princess is Pocahontas. "But she still knew how to do all kinds of neat stuff, like how to paddle a canoe, how to make leather, how to fish. . ."

Paula's dark brown eyes took on that dreamy look they always get when she talks about her favorite character.

Ella laughed. "Cinderella only knew how to keep house." She wrinkled her nose. "I'm glad I'm not *really* her. Just almost."

"What about me?" I asked. "Jasmine's main problem was that she had never been anywhere or done anything. She didn't even know how to keep house. Her servants did everything for her."

Just then a quiet tap sounded on my door. Mrs. Perth, my family's housekeeper, poked her head in. "Feel like some iced tea, girls?" she asked. She's from Scotland. Her "girls" sounded like "gells."

I blushed. "Yes, please." I'm the only one of my friends who has a full-time, live-in housekeeper. I mean, I'm glad we do, because Mrs. Perth definitely helps make our house a home. But it was too bad she had to show up right when I was talking about Jasmine's servants.

I could tell that my friends knew what I was thinking. They were grinning at me as Mrs. Perth closed the door.

"It's okay, Jasmine," said Yukiko. "We know you know how to make iced tea yourself."

"I've asked her not to wait on me like that," I grumbled.

"Oh, it's so hard being a princess," Ella said, pretending to sigh.

I gave up. There was only one thing to do. I scooped up Rajah and pointed him at my friends. "Rajah, attack!"

## Chapter Two

# How We All Met

After my friends had gone home, I wandered down to the kitchen to see if Mrs. Perth needed any help with dinner. The kitchen is my favorite room in our house. It's big and practical, and it doesn't look as decorator-y as the rest of the house. For one thing, Mrs. Perth has herbs drying all over the place. And there are bottles of oil and vinegar and jars of spaghetti.

"Hi, Mrs. P.," I said, pushing through the door. She was standing at the counter, chopping something. "Need any help?"

"No, thank you, my dear," she said with a smile.

"Everything's almost done. If you're hungry you may have some carrots and celery."

I pulled up a stool and leaned my elbows on the marble counter. I munched on a carrot. I looked around. Our kitchen is bigger than Paula's whole living room. You might as well know: I live in a mansion. Thankfully, my friends don't hold it against me. They all live in nice, regular houses.

Yukiko, Ariel, Paula, and Ella live in an area called Willow Hill. I live in Wildwood Estates. The four of them have known each other since at least kindergarten. Ariel and Paula have been best friends practically since they were in diapers. They live right around the corner from each other.

I sighed. They were the four best friends I'd ever had, and I was so glad I had met them. Two years ago, I had met Yukiko Hayashi at ballet class. We were both in the intermediate group at Madame Pavlova's Dance Academy. Yukiko was there because she loves ballet. I was there because my mom thinks ballet helps me develop poise and grace. But I like the classes anyway.

One day, when Yukiko and I were warming up at the

8

same barre, we started chatting. I found out she was a year younger than me. She was really nice, but a little shy. Over the next couple of months, we talked more and more and started hanging out at each other's houses. (Mostly mine. Yukiko's house is usually pretty noisy. That's because she has *six* brothers.)

Even though we were pretty good friends, I didn't tell her how I felt about Princess Jasmine—how I felt like I *was* her sometimes. It was a private thing. Then one day, Yukiko was joking about her six little brothers. She said, "I call them the Dwarfs—they're all smaller and younger than me. I guess that makes me Snow White."

"Oh, do you like that movie?" I asked. "It's one of my favorites."

Yukiko gave me a funny look, as if she were trying to make up her mind about something. Then she said, "You know what? My name, Yukiko, comes from the Japanese word for snow—*yuki*. And I have six brothers. It's like I really am Snow White."

When she said that, I felt a shiver go down my spine. As I looked at her, it was almost as if she turned into the real Princess Snow White, right in front of my eyes. Then

I blinked, and she was Yukiko again.

"This is so weird," I said. "You won't believe this—but have you seen the movie *Aladdin*?"

"Only about a thousand times," Yukiko said.

I held out my arms. "I'm her!" I said. "I'm Jasmine!"

Yukiko squinted at me. I knew she was looking at my long blond hair, green eyes, and freckles. She was trying to see the black hair and brown eyes of Princess Jasmine. I waited. She *had* to see it. Didn't she?

Then Yukiko's face cleared, and she smiled at me. Smiled big. "I see it!" she said. "You *are* Princess Jasmine!"

I nodded eagerly. "I'm an only child, and my parents are really rich. And they won't let me do anything because they're afraid I'll hurt myself. And I really want to go places and see things. I'm *just like* Jasmine. And my name is Jasmine, of course."

That was amazing enough, that Yukiko and I had found each other and that we each felt as if we were really Disney Princesses come to life. But it gets even more amazing.

Soon after that, Yukiko invited me over to her house. When I got there, we pushed our way through boys wrestling, boys running, and baby boys crawling and chewing on things, until we got to her room. In her room were three girls.

"Jasmine Prentiss, I'd like you to meet Ariel Ramos, Paula Pinto, and Ella O'Connor. We all go to the same school. Guys, this is Jasmine. The one I told you about."

The three other girls smiled and looked at me. I felt nervous, but I didn't know why. I looked back at them. Then . . .

"Oh, my gosh," I said slowly, staring at them.

Get this. Paula is Native American, with long black hair and brown eyes. *Pocahontas.*

Ella has dark blond hair, brown eyes, and looks a little—well—scraggly. *Cinderella.*

Ariel has long red hair and big blue eyes. *Ariel*, the Little Mermaid.

And then there was Yukiko and me. We were *all* Disney Princesses. I almost fainted.

Since then, the five of us have been best friends. I even transferred from my old school, Greenbriar Academy, to Orlando Elementary. It's like we were all made to be together, and this past year has been great. Still . . .

I finished up my carrot and sighed again.

Yukiko, Ella, Ariel, and Paula were my best friends. And I was theirs. But Yukiko and Ella were also each other's *best* best friend. And so were Ariel and Paula. Which left me by myself. What I really needed to make my life practically perfect was a *best* best friend of my very own.

# Chapter Three

# Dinner with Winthrop
# and Mary Sue

A few minutes later, Mrs. Perth rang a little brass gong in the hallway to announce dinner. (I know. Can you believe it?) My parents came down, and we went into the dining room.

(We eat breakfast in the breakfast room off the kitchen. If my parents aren't here, I eat in the kitchen with Mrs. Perth.)

Our dining room is practically the size of a bowling alley, and our table can easily seat fourteen people. My parents, Mary Sue and Winthrop Prentiss III, and I sit at one end together. Mrs. Perth puts the food in warming dishes on the sideboard, and we help ourselves. It's very fancy, but not very homelike. But it's how my parents ate when they were growing up, and how they want me to eat now. When *I'm* grown up, I'm going to have cozy family dinners around a small table, like my friends do.

Anyway. Tonight Mrs. Perth had made veal with marsala sauce, whipped potatoes, French-cut green beans, and a tossed salad with homemade dressing. It was yummy, but sometimes I wished she would make lasagna more often.

"Are you getting excited about school starting again, dear?" my mother asked.

I busily pushed some mushrooms out of the way and cut up my veal. "Yes, I can't wait. I just hope Paula and I are in the same class. But fourth grade's going to be so cool."

My mom smiled. "I was thinking that tomorrow would be a good day to go shopping," she said. "I'm sure you need some new back-to-school things."

"Um, okay," I said. Sometimes it's fun to go shopping, but I knew Mother and I had different ideas about what clothes to get. She likes frilly, expensive things from the store she buys her own clothes from. I like mix-and-match comfortable clothes with pockets. But I guessed we'd both compromise a little, and I'd end up with tons of stuff of both kinds.

I felt a warm, fuzzy body brush past my leg. Rajah. Glancing at my parents to make sure they weren't watching, I slipped him a tiny piece of veal. I almost giggled as I felt his rough little tongue take it from my fingers.

"I still can't believe they let you wear jeans to school," said Daddy. (He's from England. Mrs. Perth has been with him forever. When Daddy says "can't," it sounds like "cahn't.") "I had to wear a jacket and tie at my boarding school. Just to go to class."

I grinned at him. "Yep, I'm lucky, all right." I let another piece of veal drop to the Oriental carpet. I thought I could hear Rajah purring.

I polished off my dinner while my parents talked. (I'll eat anything and everything. I even ate snails once, when my family was in France. My friends think that's the grossest thing they've ever heard.)

"Oh, and darling," my mother said to Daddy, "Mrs. Perth said she can stay with Jasmine next week when we have that office party of yours."

15

"Oh, lovely, darling, thank you," said Daddy.

They smiled at each other, and I smiled down at my plate. My parents look like a funny match sometimes. Mother is young and very beautiful, and she likes parties and shopping and lovely things. Daddy is almost fifteen years older than she is, and a little—well—stuffy. He's a banker, after all. He likes working hard and doesn't relax very much. When he does relax, he works in our garden or listens to classical music.

But I can tell they really love each other.

"Oh, and goodness, I almost forgot," Mother said. "Guess who's coming to town, darling."

"Who's that, dear?" asked my father.

"Bunny Carlisle," Mother said happily. "My sorority sister, from college. Her husband, Trip, has been transferred here, so they've bought a place over on Maplewood Drive. I drove past it, and it's precious."

"Really? Good for them," said Daddy. He stacked up all our plates and took them to the kitchen, then came back with two slices of lemon meringue pie: one for me, one for him. My mom tries not to eat sweets.

"Best of all," Mother continued, "Bunny has a daughter just your age, Jasmine. Tiffany will be starting fourth grade at Greenbriar Academy."

For just a moment, my mom looked wistful. Greenbriar Academy is the most exclusive school in central Florida. I had gone there until last year, when I had insisted on transferring to Orlando Elementary to be with the other Disney Girls.

"You know, darling, it isn't too late to switch back," suggested my mom gently.

"Oh, no thank you," I said politely. "I'm happy at OE. But I'm sure Tiffany will like Greenbriar."

"Yes, well . . ." Mother took a sip of her black coffee. "Anyway, as soon as the Carlisles are settled, Bunny and I will get you and Tiffany together. I'm sure you'll be great friends."

I smiled and nodded. I didn't want to say that I already had great friends, but that's what I was thinking. The thing is, my parents don't really know my friends' parents that well. I guess Mother wants me to be friends with *her* friends' kids—people who have the same kind of life as we do. But I like all the other Disney Girls, and I know that what really matters is how we feel inside. Not what kind of houses we live in or what kind of cars our parents drive.

On the other hand, I thought, maybe it wouldn't be a bad thing to meet Tiffany. I mean, I was sort of looking for a best friend—I shouldn't rule anyone out. I made up my mind to give Tiffany a fair chance. With any luck, she would be great, and the other Disney Girls would like her, too, and . . .

"Ow!" my mother shrieked, jumping in her chair. Her coffee cup clattered in its saucer and spilled on the table-cloth.

Daddy and I stared at her. Then Mother turned to look at me accusingly.

Quickly I ducked my head under the table. Yep. There he was. Rajah had tried to sharpen his claws on Mother's ankle.

"May I be excused?" I asked, snatching him up quickly.

"Yes, you're excused," said Daddy. "*Both* of you."

# Chapter Four

# The First Day

"Fourth grade!" I cried, squirming in the car seat next to my mom. She turned onto the street where Orlando Elementary, my friends, and fourth grade were waiting for me.

"Fourth grade is practically fifth grade," Mother teased me.

"And fifth grade is practically sixth grade, which is middle school," I reminded her.

"You'll be heading off to college before we know it," she said. We both laughed.

Ariel, Ella, Yukiko, and Paula were waiting for me near

the front gate of OE. I jumped out of Mother's car, waved good-bye, and raced over to my friends.

"Fourth grade, here we come," Paula yelled, holding her hand up for a high five.

I smacked her hand hard, and she jumped up and down, pretending it had hurt.

"Just *third* grade seems so amazing," said Yukiko, shifting her pink flowered backpack to her other shoulder.

Ella looked at us. "I hope we're all in classes together. We'd better make a special wish," she whispered.

Yukiko nodded solemnly. I knew what Ella meant. The five of us stood in a tight circle, checking over our shoulders so that no one could see what we were doing. Then we all linked pinkie fingers and closed our eyes. Together we whispered,

> "All the magic powers that be,
> Hear us now, our special plea.
> It's us, the Disney Girls again,
> We'll make a wish, then count to ten."

Then we whispered, "Please let us all have classes together. One, two, three, four, five, six, seven, eight, nine, ten."

After we counted to ten, we opened our eyes and grinned at each other. I could practically see the magic sparkling all around us. Really.

Ariel gave an impatient bounce. "Well, let's not just stand here," she cried. "Let's go look!"

We ran over and checked the classroom lists where they were posted on the big bulletin board by the cafeteria.

"Do you see my name?" asked Yukiko anxiously, rising on tiptoe to see over the huge crush of students.

"Let me see . . . ," muttered Paula. She's the tallest, so she was peering over everyone's heads. "Yes!" she said, turning to grin at us. "You won't believe this! Jasmine and I are in Mr. Murchison's class together, 4B. And Yukiko and Ella are both in Ms. Timmons's class, 3B."

"What about me?" Ariel demanded. "Don't tell me I got mean old Mrs. Henry! By *myself*?"

Paula bit her lip and looked down at the ground.

"Oh, no!" gasped Ariel, looking horrified. "Oh, I don't believe it!"

We crowded around her, trying to think of something to make her feel better. Mrs. Henry was the worst.

Then Ariel's eyes narrowed, and she stared at Paula. I

21

looked up in time to see the corners of Paula's mouth twitch.

"You fiend!" Ariel screeched, whapping Paula on the shoulder.

Laughing, Paula raised her arms to defend herself. "Sorry, sorry," she sputtered. "Couldn't help it. You're in 3B, too."

"All right!" Ella said, jumping up and down. "We're all together! Too cool!"

When the bell rang, we split up into our two class-rooms. I was glad we wouldn't be separated into *four* different classrooms. Being in different grades is bad enough.

In Mr. Murchison's class Paula and I were assigned seats right next to each other, because our last names both start with *P:* Prentiss and Pinto. Our magic was still working! What if he had decided to seat us boy, girl, boy, girl, or something weird?

The only bad thing was that the most obnoxious boy in the whole fourth grade sat right in front of me: Kenny McIlhenny. Kenny is the class clown. Paula says he's been the class clown since kindergarten. All the boys think he's great. All us girls can't stand him. And now I had to look at his back all day, every day. Oh, well, I thought. You can't have everything.

School that day was very cool, even though we hadn't gotten Ms. Benitez. There were one or two new students, but mostly I knew everyone already. Orlando Elementary is an awesome school. It isn't as fancy as Greenbriar, where all the rooms are carpeted and there are real leather couches in the library. But I like it here much better.

Our teacher, Mr. Murchison, seemed kind of no-nonsense, but fair. Maybe he would be able to keep Kenny McIlhenny in line.

At lunchtime, Paula and I raced to the cafeteria. We saw Ella, Yukiko, and Ariel already in line ahead of us, and we waved to them. By the time Paula and I got our food, the others had sat down at our usual table: the third one down from the windows.

"You were right," Yukiko said to me. "Ms. Timmons is *so* nice."

"Paula and I sit right next to each other," I said. I opened my milk carton and put my straw in.

Ella looked down at the cafeteria lunch. "I think I'll start bringing my lunch, like I did last year."

I laughed. I didn't care what we were eating—we were all together. "Okay, everyone. Pull out your schedules," I said.

The way Orlando Elementary works is really neat. The students are divided up into grades for most classes. But for things like art, music, and gym, they lump different grades together, like third and fourth, or fourth and fifth. When we compared schedules, we found that all five of us would have art together on Mondays and Wednesdays, music together on Fridays, and gym together *every single day*!

"Oh, this is so great," Ella said happily. She closed her hand around the charm hanging from her neck and whispered, "Thank you." Each of us Disney Girls has a special magic charm—for Ella, it's a small crystal slipper. For me, it's a tiny gold lamp that I wear either around my wrist or on a necklace. Paula has a silver feather charm; Yukiko has a gold heart. Ariel has (of course) a seashell charm.

To us it is totally obvious that these charms have magic powers—especially when we use them together. You want proof? What about the gym every single day? You think that was a *coincidence*?

# Chapter Five

# Tiffany

And get this," I told Mother. "Mr. Murchison already gave us history homework. Fourth grade is going to be *so* tough. And—"

Our doorbell interrupted me. For the last hour I had been telling my mom all about my totally amazing first day. It had been great, except for Kenny McIlhenny and the fact that I still felt like I was the only Disney Girl without a *best* best friend. I could see it all now—in art class or gym, whenever we had to have partners or pair up for anything, it would be Ariel and Paula, Ella and Yukiko, and me and . . . somebody.

"Mary Sue, this is just darling," said a voice.

The Carlisles came into our living room, followed by Mrs. Perth.

Mother hugged her old sorority sister. Daddy came out of the library (yes, we have one in our house) and shook hands with Mr. Carlisle.

"My, how you've grown," Mrs. Carlisle said to me with a smile. Grown-ups always talk about how much you've grown.

"And this is Tiffany," she added.

Tiffany and I shook hands. (My parents are big on shaking hands.) I smiled at her. She had short, shiny brown hair cut in a trendy style. She was wearing a velvet dress, lace tights, and black shoes that looked like ballet slippers. She stared at me, and my smile faded. I was wearing white shorts and the T-shirt I had gotten when my parents went to Egypt. It had a picture of King Tut on it, and it said FUNKY TUT.

Tiffany looked at me like I was a worm.

During dinner I tried to ask her about her first day at Greenbriar, but she didn't seem to want to talk much. She kept sighing and pushing food around on her plate. (We were having beef Wellington, new potatoes, and asparagus. Yum.)

After dinner Mother suggested that I show Tiffany my room.

"Sure," I said, leading the way upstairs. Maybe we had just gotten off on the wrong foot. Maybe once we were away from the grown-ups, Tiffany would thaw out a little.

When I opened my door, Rajah scampered out. I picked him up and introduced him to Tiffany. She didn't smile or pet him or anything. I put him down.

Tiffany perched on my armchair while I sprawled over the end of my bed. She looked around my room and gave a little yawn.

I looked around to see what was so boring. My mom redecorates my room every two or three years, and usually the only thing I get to pick out is the sheets. This year the whole room was in shades of green and pink, with pale green carpet, pink striped wallpaper with a floral border, and matching curtains. I have a double-size four-poster bed with a canopy. By the windows, there's an armchair and a chaise longue with a small table between them.

Across from my bed is an armoire that holds my TV, VCR, and CD player. I also have, next to my bed, a small Oriental carpet in shades of rose and pine green. You guessed it. It's my magic carpet.

My friends all love my room. I have to say, it *is* pretty. It's big and sunny. But it doesn't feel like *me*, you know? (Except for my special rug.) It feels more like my mom. Which isn't exactly a bad thing. But my friends have bedrooms that really seem like them. Someday I will, too.

"So," I said. "Where did you move from?"

"Washington, D.C." Tiffany looked sad just saying it.

"Did you like it there?" I kicked off my shoes. Rajah immediately pounced on one and started chewing on the laces. He's so-o-o cute.

"Oh, *yeah*," Tiffany said, perking up. "It was fabulous. There was always so much to do, like museums and shopping and everything. And we lived in this great town house right in the city, and Mom and I could hop on the subway and go places." She stopped and frowned. "Not like it is here."

I knew what she meant. Orlando is pretty big, but it

isn't as sophisticated as New York or Paris or even Washington, D.C.

"But there are a lot of great things here," I said. "I feel so lucky living practically right next door to Walt Disney World. And there's always tons of stuff to do. . ."

Tiffany snorted. At least it sounded like a little snort.

"It's so *hot* here. This is September. It's much too hot. And it's so flat. There are no pretty hills. And do not even get me started about the *mosquitoes*." She crossed her arms over her chest.

I blinked. Maybe it would just take Tiffany a while to get used to Orlando. There are so many great things about living here—I could go on all day. But I could tell she wasn't in the mood to hear them.

"Want to watch TV?" I asked.

"Sure," said Tiffany, without much enthusiasm.

So we watched some dumb show on TV until her parents called her. To tell you the truth, I don't watch a lot of TV. I like to read instead.

After Tiffany left, I did my homework, then got ready for bed. Mother came in to kiss me good night.

"Tiffany seems pretty unhappy about moving," I told her.

Mother sat on the edge of my bed and smoothed my hair with her hand. "I know. Maybe you can help her be happier here. Bunny has signed her up for ballet classes at Madame Pavlova's. We've arranged for you two to carpool together."

I groaned to myself. Great. By now I was pretty sure that Tiffany and I would never be best friends. We would probably never be any kind of friends at all.

"And I thought it would be nice if you invited Tiffany over this Saturday to swim," my mom continued.

"I've already asked my friends over," I said.

"Tiffany can join you, can't she?" asked my mom. I knew it wasn't really a question.

"Yeah, I guess," I said.

Mother smiled and kissed me. "Good. Thanks. Now sleep well, darling."

After she left, Rajah and I snuggled up together. I was really, really tired. I started thinking about Princess Jasmine from *Aladdin*, and I wondered what she would do about Tiffany. I saw myself in Jasmine's garden at the palace. I was wearing her clothes and my hair was long and black. Then I heard the doors open to the garden.

My mother's voice said, "I think Jasmine is out there, Tiffany, darling." Quickly I climbed over the garden wall and escaped out into the town to meet my real friends.

I fell asleep with a smile on my face.

# Chapter Six

# The New Girl

Before class the next morning, I was telling Paula about Tiffany. Paula and I were putting our books away and getting ready for first period, which was reading comprehension.

"And then Rajah climbed up my bedspread and got stuck, and I had to go unhook him," I said. Paula laughed. She loves animals and always likes to hear about the latest cute thing Rajah has done. "And Tiffany didn't even smile," I continued.

"Hmm. Maybe she just doesn't like cats," said Paula mildly.

"But Mother wants me to be nice to her, so I guess I have to be," I said. "At least until she finds some new friends at Greenbriar."

"She'll probably feel more settled in soon," Paula said. That's Paula for you. She can always see both sides to every question. And she always tries to be fair, no matter what. It's one of the great things about her. "Oh, guess what," she continued, "Damon says he'll help me with my soccer moves this weekend." (Damon is Paula's big brother.)

Just then Mr. Murchison came in. We quit talking. I sat looking at the back of Kenny McIlhenny's head.

After Mr. Murchison took roll call, we threw ourselves into reading comprehension. Fourth grade isn't like third grade. Fourth grade is all business—work, work, work.

We were in the middle of second period—spelling— when the door opened. The school secretary, Ms. Kamai, had a new girl with her. Mr. Murchison went over to talk to them, and then Ms. Kamai left.

"Class," said Mr. Murchison, "this is a new student. Her name is Isabelle Beaumont."

Isabelle stood there looking a little shy. She was African

American, with short, curly black hair. She was small and slender, like me. Her skin was a pretty, creamy brown, and she had really big dark brown eyes. She looked nice, I thought.

"Isabelle has just transferred here from the Janet Gregory School," added Mr. Murchison. "I know you'll all help her feel welcome here in 4B."

"Ha! Fat chance," said Kenny McIlhenny loudly. "We don't need her here. Tell her to transfer again, into 4A."

Paula and I stared at each other in shock. We couldn't believe even Kenny would be so mean to a new girl.

But Isabelle just rolled her eyes. "Hush up, Kenny," she said. "No one's interested in your lame opinion."

Paula and I stared at each other again, this time with smiles on our faces. Obviously Isabelle knew Kenny. And as the saying goes, to know Kenny is to dislike him.

Mr. Murchison put Isabelle in the first row, since her name started with a *B*. I couldn't wait to talk to her.

When the lunch bell rang, everyone leaped out of his or her seat and raced to the door. Everyone except the new girl. She sat at her desk, looking unsure of herself.

Paula and I went over to her. "Hi, I'm Jasmine

Prentiss," I said. "And this is Paula Pinto. Do you know where the cafeteria is?"

Isabelle smiled shyly. "Not yet. Can I go with you?"

"Sure," said Paula.

That day at lunch, Isabelle sat with us DGs at our usual table.

"I've lived in Orlando my whole life," she told us. "But my parents felt the Janet Gregory School wasn't challenging enough, so they transferred me here."

"How do you know Kenny?" asked Paula.

Isabelle wiped her mouth with her napkin and groaned. "He's my next-door neighbor," she explained. "We live in Willow Hill. Not only that, but his parents and my parents are best friends."

"Oh, gee, I'm sorry," said Ella.

"Me, too," said Isabelle, grinning. "Once I even had to go on vacation with Kenny."

Ariel gasped and patted Isabelle's hand.

"It's funny," said Paula. "But you know, we all live in Willow Hill, too. Except for Jasmine."

(It would be so fun if I lived in Willow Hill, with everyone else.)

"This is great," said Isabelle happily. "I was kind of nervous about starting a new school. I'm so glad to meet you guys, right from my own neighborhood."

I smiled at her. "It can be hard, starting all over," I said. "I transferred here last year. But as soon as you begin meeting people, it makes everything better."

Isabelle nodded. "Yeah. So far this school seems okay. Mr. Murchison seems pretty decent. And you guys have a great library! My old school's library was much smaller and not very up-to-date."

"Oh, do you like books?" I asked.

Laughing, Isabelle pushed her lunch tray away. "I *love* books! I read all the time. It's my favorite thing to do."

Then we all started talking about what our favorite books were. Before we knew it, the lunch bell rang again.

"See you in art class," I told Ella, Yukiko, and Ariel.

The rest of the afternoon, Paula and I helped Isabelle find her way around as much as we could. By the end of day, she seemed much more comfortable.

After school, we waited together for our rides. (My mother was picking me up. The others usually took the school bus.)

"It was great meeting you all today," said Isabelle. "You sure made my first day a lot easier than I thought it would be. Thanks."

"No problem," I said as I saw Mother's car pull up. "See you tomorrow."

I left Isabelle in the hands of the other Disney Girls. I was glad she was in our class.

Chapter Seven

# Swimming with Tiffany

Some people wake up to alarm clocks. I wake up because Rajah starts licking my face with his rough little tongue.

On Saturday morning I tried to push him away. "Ugh, cat breath," I groaned. He purred and licked my nose.

As if that weren't enough, as soon as I opened my eyes I remembered that today was TS day: Tiffany Swimming day. I sighed. Thursday's ballet class at Madame Pavlova's had been kind of a drag.

Tiffany had thought Madame Pavlova treated us like babies. At her old class in Washington, D.C., she had

already been in toe shoes and was doing *sauts de chat.*
Blah, blah, blah. She had complained the whole time. It
had taken all the fun out of it for me and Yukiko—and
probably everyone else, too.

Now I had to spend the whole afternoon with her. I
jumped out of bed and threw on some jeans shorts and a
white T-shirt with pink rosebuds and fake pearls sewn all
around the neck.

At least I wouldn't have to deal with Tiffany alone.
Ariel, Yukiko, Paula, and Ella were going to show up
around eleven. Not only that, but I had asked Isabelle
Beaumont to come over, too. The six of us could handle
one Tiffany, couldn't we?

"This dip is great," said Ella, swiping her chip.

"Tell Mrs. Perth," I said. "She made everything. But I
helped."

"Could you put some sunscreen on my shoulders?"
Paula asked.

"Sure," said Ariel.

"Tiffany, do you need more lemonade?" I asked
politely.

Tiffany looked down at her glass. "No, thanks," she said. "Back home, everyone drank mixed drinks like ginger ale and peach juice. Or pineapple juice and seltzer."

"I *love* this lemonade," said Isabelle. "There's nothing better on a hot day." She held out her glass for a refill, and I smiled at her.

"*Every* day is a hot day here," Tiffany complained. "Back home, it would almost be time for the leaves to start changing. The trees turn red and gold, and people start having fires in their fireplaces."

For a moment I felt sorry for her. She really missed her old home. On the other hand, complaining about *my* home didn't exactly help anything.

"That sounds great," said Yukiko, trying to be friendly. "It must be hard to start over in such a different kind of place."

"But sometimes a change can be really good," said Isabelle. "I mean, I always felt like I didn't really fit in at my old school. But maybe Orlando Elementary will be better for me."

"Well, I don't exactly think Orlando is going to be a

step up for *me*," said Tiffany. She looked away from us and put on her sunglasses.

I didn't know what to do or say. We had been trying to be nice to Tiffany, but she wasn't trying back.

"Try to look at it this way," said Paula. "When it's freezing in Washington, and snowing and icy, everyone up there will be jealous of you, lounging by your pool in February."

Tiffany didn't even answer her.

I sent a message to Ariel with my eyes. *Do something.*

Leaping up, Ariel ran to the diving board. "I know!" she said. "Let's play follow-the-leader. Everyone has to do everything I do. Okay?"

Paula looked at her suspiciously. "Like what?"

"Like this!" Ariel ran to the end of the diving board, bounced hard once, then did a perfect somersault into the water. She bobbed up, pushed her hair out of her eyes, and motioned to the rest of us. "Come on! One flip, then sidestroke across the pool." She swam expertly to the shallow end.

Yukiko, Ella, and Paula laughed and ran to the diving board. I shrugged at Isabelle.

"Ready?" I asked her.

"Ready and willing, but I don't know if I'm *able*," she said. But she ran to get in line behind Paula. Yukiko did a flip, then starting swimming the sidestroke over to Ariel. Ella tried to do a flip, but belly flopped and came up sputtering.

I looked over at Tiffany to urge her to join us, but she was reading a magazine, not even looking at us.

"She just needs more time to get used to it here," said Isabelle softly.

"She's being a total drag," I whispered angrily.

"Don't let her ruin your day," Isabelle said. She gave me a big smile. "*I'm* having a wonderful time. I love your yard, and your pool, and everything."

Suddenly I felt a lot better. "Thanks." Isabelle and I dived into the pool.

"Okay, now swim underwater as far as you can!" Ariel shouted. She took a deep breath and slipped underwater with hardly any splash.

"She has the perfect name," laughed Isabelle. "She really does swim like a mermaid."

My ears pricked up. So far, Isabelle was really nice,

really smart, and really fun. If she was as crazy about Disney movies as I was, she would be practically perfect.

"Oh, do you like *The Little Mermaid*?" I asked her.

"Oh, yeah," said Isabelle. "It was great." Then she held her nose and went underwater.

Hmm, I thought.

After everyone left, I sat by the pool, thinking. I felt worn out. Tiffany had been yucky. Isabelle had been great. Maybe . . . could Isabelle be the one? Could she somehow become my very own *best* best friend?

Then I frowned. But how? We five Disney Girls were more than just best friends. We had something really special—and secret—in common. Each of us just *was* a Disney Princess, deep down inside ourselves. Could I teach Isabelle to be one? Or do you have to be born to it? Would Isabelle even want to be a Disney Girl? What if she just didn't get it? And most important—what would the other girls say?

# Chapter Eight

# Odd Girl Out

Watch it, watch it—this turn's sharp!" Ariel yelled. She tucked down into a speed skater's crouch and expertly whipped around a hairpin curve.

Paula hunkered down and raced right after her.

Ella, Yukiko, and I followed them as they got farther and farther ahead. Ariel and Paula are more athletic than the rest of us. Or maybe they're just more daring. Anyway, they were zipping around like roller-derby queens, leaving us in their dust.

"This is a beautiful park," I said. "You guys are lucky to live so close."

The Willow Hill suburb has its very own park, called Willow Green. It isn't huge, but there are bike and skating paths, a small fountain, a bandstand, and some little snack shops. The five of us often meet here on the weekends and go skating or bicycling, or we just hang out and play Frisbee.

Around and around the park we skated. Ariel and Paula passed Yukiko, Ella, and me about a dozen times. Finally we flagged them down.

"Let's get something to drink," I called. Paula and Ariel skidded to a stop. Even though I hadn't been skating very fast, I was hot and sweaty anyway. Here in Orlando, the air is usually so warm and humid that when you sweat, it doesn't even evaporate. You just stay sweaty. Gross, huh? Some days I take three showers.

We all bought frozen lemonades and plunked down on a long bench.

"Perfect," Ariel sighed. Her long red hair was in three limp, messy braids hanging down her back. Her pale skin was flushed, and she was still breathing hard.

"Nothing's better than frozen lemonade," Paula agreed, slurping some up with a straw.

For a few minutes we just worked on our lemonades, soaking up the sunshine and letting the breeze cool us off.

"Oh, look," whispered Ella, pointing. "It's Drizella and Anastasia."

We looked to where she was pointing and saw two older girls arguing as they bought some cotton candy. They looked grumpy and unfriendly, and we all giggled. We love to match real people up with characters from our favorite movies.

"I thought Drizella and Anastasia lived at home with you," said Yukiko.

Ella groaned. Her father had gotten remarried recently, and Ella was having a hard time adjusting to her new stepmother and two new stepsisters. "Don't remind me," she said.

I was quiet for a while, as the others matched up more characters. Yukiko knew about Ella's feelings a little more than the rest of us, because she was Ella's best friend. And Ariel and Paula were wearing the exact same kind of in-line skates. They had gone to buy them together—because they were best friends. And here I was, the girl alone. Friends with everyone, best friends with no one.

I sighed.

"What's the matter, Jasmine?" asked Paula. Her warm brown eyes looked at me with concern.

I hadn't meant to sigh so loud. Shaking my head, I said, "Oh, nothing."

"Are you sure?" asked Ariel. "You've been kind of quiet all day."

"Next to you, *anyone* seems quiet," teased Ella.

Ariel made a face at her, then turned back to me.

"No, really, I'm fine," I said quickly. "Maybe I'm just worried about school. Mr. Murchison is giving a lot of homework."

"Listen, I'll come over and study with you," said Paula. "It'd be good for me, too. Okay?"

I smiled at her. It's true that I don't have a *best* best friend, but I do have four of the best friends that anyone could ask for. "Thanks," I said. "That would be great."

Right then a girl walking by caught my eye. It was Isabelle, but she hadn't seen us. Mainly because she was walking and reading a book at the same time.

I jumped up happily. "Isabelle, hi! Isabelle!"

Finally she heard me and looked up. She glanced

around, then saw us and waved. Smiling, she walked over. "Hi, guys. It's a great day to go skating. Do you come here a lot?"

"Uh-huh." I nodded.

"I do, too," said Isabelle. "It's funny we haven't noticed each other before. I come here all the time."

It's no wonder you didn't notice us, I thought, if you walk around with your nose buried in a book!

"We'll definitely call you the next time we come," I said. "Then we can all go together."

"Great!" Isabelle looked pleased. I wondered if the other Disney Girls would mind if we included her with us more often.

"I live over on Hampson Street," said Paula. "Right around the corner from Ariel, on Dublin. Ella lives on Sherman Drive, and Yukiko lives right up the street, on Homestead."

"Homestead and what?" asked Isabelle.

"Homestead and Franklin," said Yukiko.

"Oh, my gosh!" said Isabelle. "I live on Franklin, two blocks up from Homestead."

And *moi*? I live way over at Wildwood Estates. Sigh.

While we were chatting, Isabelle glanced away and smiled.

"Did you see someone you know?" I asked.

"No—but that guy over there, next to the lemonade stand . . ." Isabelle pointed. "He looks exactly like Lefou, from *Beauty and the Beast*."

My heart started pounding. Isabelle matched up people with characters from Disney movies, too! Was it possible that she could somehow learn to be a Disney Girl?

# Chapter Nine

# Shopping with Isabelle

I asked Isabelle to eat lunch with us on Monday and Tuesday.

"Are you sure?" she asked. "I don't want to butt in on you guys."

"Don't be silly," I said breezily. "Of course we want you to sit with us." I hadn't asked the others if it was okay—to tell you the truth, I didn't want to take the chance that they would say it wasn't. But *I* wanted Isabelle to sit with us. So she did.

At lunchtime I noticed that it wasn't as easy for the five

of us to talk when Isabelle was there. For one thing, we couldn't talk about being Disney Princesses or any of the special things that go along with that. So we just talked about school, and books, and stuff like that.

"My sneakers are about to wear out," I said. "Anyone want to go to the mall tomorrow with me?" Before anyone could answer, I turned to Isabelle. "Do you think you could go?" I asked.

Out of the corner of my eye, I saw Ella and Yukiko exchange a glance. But Isabelle was saying, "Yeah, I think I probably could. I have to ask my mom, but I need a new pair of sneakers, too."

"Great!" I said. "Anyone else?"

"I can't," said Ariel. "Swim practice."

"I promised Mom I'd help her in the yard," said Paula.

"Me, neither," Yukiko said, shaking her head.

"I can't go, either," said Ella. "Sorry."

"Oh. Well, it's just you and me, then, Isabelle," I said. I was already looking forward to it.

On Wednesday afternoon, Mother gave me a ride to the Southland Mall. I was supposed to meet Isabelle at the fountain right in the middle of the main hall.

"Okay, dear," said my mom. "I'm going to run over to the Gigi shop and see if they have anything new. I'll meet you at the entrance to Jordan's at four-thirty, right?"

"Right," I said. She kissed me and headed off to her favorite store.

"Jasmine!" Isabelle called. I turned to see her waving good-bye to her mother, who headed off in another direction.

"Hey," I said, smiling. "That was your mom, right?"

"Yeah," said Isabelle. "She's taking the afternoon off. She owns her own gourmet food shop, but she has a manager who can run things for her."

"Great," I said. "My mom's at Gigi's. You'll probably meet her later. You want to go to Best Foot Forward to look at sneakers?"

"Sure," said Isabelle.

Shopping with Isabelle was majorly fun. Every time we passed a window, we stopped and looked. And we always liked the exact same things! On our way to Best Foot Forward, we stopped at the bookstore and looked at all the new books in the kids' section. Isabelle told me about a great new series she was reading, and she offered to lend me the first two. I showed her one of my favorite books, about a girl who lives by herself on an island, and Isabelle said she'd like to borrow it.

It was like we were sisters or something.

At Best Foot Forward, we both reached for the same sneaker at the same time.

"This one is really pretty," I said.

"It would go with anything, and it's on sale," agreed Isabelle. We grinned at each other.

Then we bought the *exact same sneakers*. Just like Ariel and Paula had the same skates. I was in heaven.

We ended up at the food court. I got an ice-cream cone, and Isabelle got a dish of hummus and some pita chips from the Middle Eastern place.

"I love this stuff," she said. "Mom sells it in her shop, and I eat it all the time. She's introduced me to all sorts of new foods."

"I love to try new things, too," I said happily. "Last week I had squid sushi. But I never even thought of getting the hummus here. Maybe next time."

Isabelle smiled. "Here, we can share."

I looked down at my ice-cream cone. Suddenly it looked too sweet and not very satisfying. I ate it quickly, then tried a little hummus. It was delicious.

"Have you ever tried the falafel here?" I was asking Isabelle when suddenly something hit my left ear. "Hey!" I looked down to see a paper straw wrapper float to the floor.

"Oh, no," Isabelle groaned. "It's the Beast." She jerked her thumb over to where Kenny McIlhenny was sitting a few tables away.

"Knock it off, Kenny," I ordered him, but he just made a face at me.

"Try to ignore him," advised Isabelle, but I noticed she was carefully drawing her own straw out of its wrapper.

"Why do you call him the Beast?" I asked. I had a feeling I already knew.

"Because he's such a total pain," said Isabelle. "He's rude, and loud, and can't get along with anybody. You know, like the Beast in *Beauty and the Beast*."

That was the second time she had mentioned that movie.

"He gets along with other boys," I pointed out. I got

my own straw wrapper ready. Just then a wadded-up napkin landed on our table. Isabelle and I picked up our wrappers.

"Other boys don't count," said Isabelle, raising her wrapper to her lips. "I meant that he can't get along with anybody important. Like girls."

"One, two, three," I whispered. "Now!"

At the same time, we whirled and blew our straw wrappers at Kenny the Beast as hard as we could. He jerked in surprise as mine hit him right in the forehead. Isabelle's went into his open mouth! We both laughed so hard we almost fell off our seats.

Kenny spit the wrapper out angrily. "I'll get you back!" he warned us. "Just you wait." Then he stomped off.

Laughing, we slapped high fives.

It seemed like much too soon that we had to go meet our mothers. On the way to Jordan's, I remembered what I wanted to ask Isabelle.

"You know, you've mentioned *Beauty and the Beast* a couple times," I said. "Is that your favorite movie?"

Isabelle looked a little flustered.

"Um, yeah, sure, I guess," she said. Then she pointed at

the window of Tootsie's Delight. "Hey! Look at those cute shoes!"

The shoes *were* cute, but I thought Isabelle had changed the subject on purpose. Why?

# Chapter Ten

# Lovely Autumn Leaves

She's just really cool," I told Yukiko softly. We were warming up at the barre on Thursday afternoon. Madame Pavlova's assistant, Mademoiselle Sandra, was walking up and down, correcting a foot position here, an arm movement there.

"Yeah," Yukiko agreed in a whisper. We moved into the fifth position. "I like Isabelle, too. It sure does seem like you're spending a lot of time with her."

For a second I felt almost guilty. I *was* seeing Isabelle pretty often. We just really clicked. But was I ignoring my other friends? I frowned as we started across the room to practice jetés.

As my class formed three lines, I thought about being one of the Disney Girls and how important it was to me. It was like my life had been missing something before I met those four girls, whom I could share my biggest secret feelings with. But I was really enjoying spending time with Isabelle, too. If only Isabelle could be a Disney Girl somehow! That would be a miracle. Or maybe just magical . . .

"Hi," said Tiffany briskly. I had almost forgotten that she was in our ballet class.

"Hi, Tiffany," I said.

"Would you like to come over to my house on Monday afternoon, after school?" Tiffany asked me with gritted teeth.

I groaned inside. I could tell that her mom had made her ask me. And I knew that *my* mom would make me go. Our mothers really wanted us to be friends. But we could hardly stand each other!

I sighed. "Sure, Tiffany, thanks," I said. I didn't want to go any more than she wanted to ask me.

"Great," she said. She sounded as if she thought it wasn't great at all. But what could we do? "See you then."

Tiffany went and stood in another line, and I leaped across the room in a series of jetés.

"Now, class," said Mademoiselle Sandra, "today we will have a new exercise. I will play a piece of music called 'Autumn.' You may dance however you want, while thinking about autumn and the way it makes you feel. Think of crisp days, falling leaves, new apples, and anything else that says autumn to you."

"In Orlando autumn means swimming parties, shorts, hot days, and frozen lemonade," Yukiko whispered behind me. I had to hide my smile behind my hand.

Mademoiselle Sandra started the music. For a few moments we all stood around, waiting for inspiration. I listened to the music and tried to think autumny thoughts. I closed my eyes.

Slowly, I heard the music change. I began to think of round white towers and small keyhole-shaped windows. I heard the trickling of a fountain and the soft cooing of lovebirds kept as pets. Then I knew: I was at the palace, Jasmine's palace. My palace. My magic carpet was waiting for me, and I climbed on. Where would it take me? My arms lifted as I felt the carpet swirl me into the air. I opened my eyes and pictured exotic, far-off countries flying far below me. I swirled and dipped and leaped around our studio as my magic carpet whisked me to wonderful places I had never imagined.

Finally the music faded and stopped. I drifted down to earth and felt Jasmine's world slowly dissolve. I blinked and saw Mademoiselle Sandra smiling at me.

"That was quite lovely, my dear," she said. "I believe you and Yukiko both really felt the spirit of the music." She walked gracefully over to the CD player to change the music.

"What were you thinking about?" I asked Yukiko.

"I was imagining that I was lost in the forest after the gamekeeper told me to run away," replied Yukiko softly. I knew the scene from *Snow White* that she was talking about. "The wind was tearing at my clothes, and I was getting caught on branches. I just whirled this way and that, trying to escape."

See what I mean? Being a Disney Girl made special things like this happen to us all the time.

After class Yukiko and I changed back into our school clothes. I was talking to Yukiko about a field trip that our school was going to take next week. We were going to Walt Disney World! A group of international dancers was going to perform at EPCOT, and practically everyone at Orlando Elementary had signed up to go.

"And you know what? I'm going to ask Isabelle to be my partner for the field trip," I said. People always have to have a field-trip buddy at our school. So you don't get lost or something.

Yukiko silently laced up her brown granny boots.

"What?" I asked her.

She turned her dark brown eyes to me. "Look," she said hesitantly. "I like Isabelle as much as you do. But—she isn't really *like us*, you know?" Yukiko lowered her voice and looked around to make sure no one was listening. "I mean, the five of us all . . . have something special in common. You know what I mean."

I crossed my arms over my chest. "So what are you saying? You guys don't want me to be friends with Isabelle?"

"No, of course not," said Yukiko quickly. She stood up and stuffed her leotard and tights into her gym bag. "It's just—I guess I'm worried that you'll start to like Isabelle more than you like us."

"That would be impossible," I said. "It's just that I like Isabelle, and I need a field-trip buddy. That's all."

Yukiko looked relieved as we walked out of the ballet school. But now I felt worried. Would I have to choose between Isabelle—who might possibly be my *best* best friend someday—and the Disney Girls?

# Chapter Eleven

# Uptown Friday Night

"Pass the egg rolls, please," said Paula.

Ella pushed the carton down the kitchen counter to her. It was Friday night, and we were having a sleepover at my house. Every few weeks we take turns hosting them. I have to admit, my friends love it when it's my turn. For one thing, my parents always let us get take-out food. Tonight we were having Chinese. We had all decided to use chopsticks. Only Yukiko and I could actually get any food into our mouths.

"May I please have a dinglehopper, before I starve to

death?" Ariel complained. Little pieces of food littered her place mat.

"You know where we keep our dinglehoppers," I said, waving a chopstick at our silverware drawer. "Just don't try to comb your hair with it, like in your movie."

Everyone laughed.

After dinner we went swimming. Swimming at night is really cool. My dad turns on the underwater lights, and the whole pool glows like a magical cavern.

One by one we leaped into the balmy water, seeing it splash whitely around us. It was comfortable being us five again. We didn't have to watch what we said. We could be Disney Princesses without worrying about what anyone would think of us.

On the other hand, I missed Isabelle. Sleepovers are always fun, but they're really private, too. I knew the DGs would have been uncomfortable if I had asked Isabelle to come. Could she have fit in somehow? Would she have fun doing the things we do? Could I be happy as a Disney Girl if Isabelle couldn't join in?

"Okay, I'm a shark," called Ariel, clapping her hands. "You guys are mermaids. Better swim fast!"

Yukiko squealed and leaped away from Ariel. Ariel plunged into the water, making snapping motions with her hands, as if they were giant jaws.

"I'm a shark, too," said Paula, grinning ferociously at me.

I yelped and threw myself toward the shallow end, swimming as fast as I could. We were sharks and mermaids for hours. Then Ariel was Princess Ariel, and the rest of us were other mermaids in her kingdom. We had singing concerts, escaped from the evil Sea Witch, Ursula, and stuff like that. I threw some pennies to the bottom of the shallow end, and we pretended they were treasures from a sunken ship. We lost ourselves in Ariel's beautiful underwater world, and it was wonderful. I wondered what Isabelle would say if I told her about this.

For just a minute, I imagined that Isabelle was here with us now. I saw her smiling and laughing and splashing through the water. She seemed just as much a Disney Girl as the rest of us. But who was she?

Just then, I realized Yukiko was saying my name.

"Earth to Jasmine," she said. "Please come in."

I smiled. "Sorry. Is it my turn?" I dove beneath the water.

Later we floated on our backs, gazing up at the stars in the sky. It was beautiful and clear. I could practically feel the magic glowing around me and my four best friends.

After swimming, we were all hungry enough to eat a whale. We loaded up with popcorn and ice-cream bars and went to my playroom on the third floor. Rajah trotted up the steps after us.

"Pick a movie, any movie," said Ella.

Of course we always watch our favorite movies at these sleepovers. I closed my eyes and grabbed one off the shelf.

"Huh. *Beauty and the Beast*," I said, popping it in the VCR. "We haven't watched this one in a while."

We all got comfy as Belle walked through her small town, singing about how she didn't fit in. I frowned. Belle reminded me of someone—something someone had said. But I couldn't remember what it was. Anyway, it was a great movie, and we were all glad to see it again.

Much later I lay awake in the darkness. My friends were asleep in their sleeping bags on the playroom floor. Rajah was curled up on the bottom of my sleeping bag, his paws covering his face.

It had been a majorly fun evening. We always have great

times together. So why wasn't I happy? I felt so confused.

Very quietly I sneaked out of the playroom. Downstairs in my own room, I opened my jewelry box. I took out my special magical charm, the gold lamp, and held it in my hand. Then I sat crosslegged on the small Oriental carpet by my bed and closed my eyes. I cupped my tiny lamp in both hands.

"All the magic powers that be,
Hear me now, my special plea.
It's me, a princess, calling you,
Help me know what I should do."

The lamp in my hands began to feel warm. Glancing down, I could see it practically glowing between my fingers. In my mind I pictured Isabelle and the rest of the Disney Girls. It was as if they were on a seesaw, with Isabelle on one side and everyone else on the other. Slowly, the seesaw tilted until the two sides were even.

I let my mind drift, thinking about our sleepover and the movie we had watched. What had that movie reminded me of? Who . . . ? I saw Belle again, walking through the streets in her small village, feeling as if she didn't belong. Who had said that? Who had I seen

68

recently, walking and reading a book at the same time? Some real person.

"Ow!" I whispered, dropping the charm. It glowed brightly on the swirling pattern of the rug. I touched it—it was still hot. Then it came to me—Belle! Isabelle! Isabelle was just like Belle, in *Beauty and the Beast*! I had seen Isabelle walking and reading a book at the same time, in the park at Willow Hill. At the time I had thought it was funny. Now it was kind of eerie, the way it seemed so much like Belle.

Not only that, but Isabelle had mentioned not belonging at her other school. Not fitting in. *And* there was the whole Kenny McIlhenny thing—the Beast. As I sat on my magic carpet, clue after clue came to me. I grabbed up my charm and put it safely away. Then I slipped silently upstairs to the playroom. Once again, the magic had come through for me. I knew who Isabelle was. And I knew what I had to do.

Chapter Twelve

# Enough Already, Tiffany!

I knew what I was going to do—but I wasn't sure when I should do it. And to tell you the truth, it seemed like such a humongously big deal that I kind of got cold feet for a few days.

All day on Monday at school, I felt as if I were watching everyone from behind a magic mirror. What would Isabelle say? What would Paula, Yukiko, Ella, and Ariel say? What would *I* say? The tension was killing me.

On top of everything, I had to go over to Tiffany Carlisle's house that Monday afternoon. Her mom picked me up and drove me to their new house, which was only about eight blocks from my house in Wildwood Estates.

"I'm so happy you could come over today," said Mrs. Carlisle, giving me a big smile. I smiled back.

Inside, their house was about as big as ours. They had a pool, too, and a huge kitchen, and stuff like that. Most of their furniture was in place, but there were still big piles of boxes and unopened crates.

"Forgive the mess," said Tiffany's mother. "I can't do a thing until my decorator gets back from London."

I nodded.

Their housekeeper fixed us a snack, and we went up to Tiffany's room. Her room was a lot like mine, but in different colors. It looked all designer-y and grown-up.

We ate our snack in silence, not looking at each other. Tiffany put a CD into her player. It was a Casey Brothers album, and I like the Casey Brothers. But I was pretty darn bored. I sighed. She sighed. We didn't talk.

Sitting in her beanbag chair, I wondered how long I had to stay before I could call my mom and ask her to pick me up. I was playing with my hair, staring off into space, when suddenly I heard a muffled snorfling sound. I looked at Tiffany in surprise.

She was crying! She was half-sitting, half-lying on her flowered bedspread. Her hands covered her face, and her shoulders were shaking. Tiffany, crying! I didn't know what to do.

So I just did what I would do for any of my friends. I got up, went over, and patted her shoulder. "Tiffany," I said worriedly. "What's the matter?"

For a few long moments she didn't answer me. I handed her a tissue from a box next to her bed. She wiped her eyes and sat up a little.

"I'm so unhappy here!" she blurted. "I just want to be back home again, with all my old friends. If I were sitting here with Marcy or Jessica, I would be so happy. We could listen to the Casey Brothers, and talk, and read magazines, and watch TV. But instead I'm sitting here with you, in Florida!" She started to cry again.

Okay, so she had just insulted me. But I didn't take it personally. How could I? I knew exactly how she felt. I didn't like being here with her, either. I would be much happier myself if I could be here listening to the Casey Brothers with any of my other friends.

Sitting next to Tiffany on her bed, I patted her shoulder some more. (I don't know why that helps, but it does.)

"I'm sorry, Tiffany," I said. "I know how you feel. You had to leave behind everything and everyone you knew. Now you have to start all over again."

She nodded and sniffled. "I don't have any friends at my new school," she admitted. "Some of them seem nice, but I'm still an outsider. All I have is you. And I don't even like you."

I couldn't help it—I started to laugh. At least Tiffany was being honest. When she realized what she had said, she looked embarrassed. Then she started to laugh a little, too.

"Sorry. I just meant we don't have anything in common."

"I know what you meant," I said. "Listen, starting over is hard—but a few friends will help you get through anything. Hey, I know! I used to go to Greenbriar until just a year and a half ago. I still talk to some of the girls sometimes. Why don't I call up a few and tell them you're a friend of mine? Then they'll probably make an extra effort to help you."

Tiffany sniffled again and stopped crying. "You think so?"

"I bet it would help," I said.

"You don't mind?"

"Nope. I'll call them tonight," I promised.

At last Tiffany smiled and wiped her tears away. "Thanks," she said. "I would appreciate it."

By the time I left that day, both Tiffany and I felt much better. In a way, we liked each other better, now that we had admitted we really didn't like each other. It sounds weird, but it's true.

And we knew that from now on, we could get together often enough to make our mothers happy. But we didn't have to be real friends. The pressure was off.

I hummed a little song all the way home.

Chapter Thirteen

# The Land of the Mouse

Since I live in Orlando, I've been to Walt Disney World dozens of times. But I still get so excited about going that I can hardly sit still. It's truly a magical place. There's always something new to see or do, or something I haven't noticed before. All of us DGs wish we could live there.

For our field trip, our teachers lumped grades together: first and second, third and fourth, fifth and sixth. Which meant we could all choose each other as field-trip buddies. Ariel and Paula were partners, Ella was with Yukiko, and Isabelle and I paired up. It was wonderful to be with my five favorite people, all at the same time. I was practically bouncing in my seat when the school buses let us off at the gates to EPCOT.

"Now, remember, kids," warned Mr. Murchison. "You have one hour to explore EPCOT before the performance begins in France at one o'clock. I expect to see all of you with your partners on time. Do not be late. Remember the safety rules we discussed. And have a good time."

"Yay!" I yelled as we ran out into the wide world of EPCOT. About a hundred feet later, we stopped.

"What should we do first?" asked Yukiko.

"I wish we could go to the Magic Kingdom right now," said Ella. "But it's great that we'll be able to spend two hours there after the performance."

"I'm starving," said Ariel. "Why don't we go to Mexico and get something to eat?"

We all laughed.

"You *always* say that when we come here," I said. I turned to Isabelle and explained, "Ariel burns off so much energy that she's always hungry. And her favorite food is Mexican."

Paula waved her hand. "Do you remember that time Ariel made us search the entire Magic Kingdom for

Mexican food because she had a craving?"

Ariel didn't even look embarrassed. "Hey, I know what I like. But if you guys don't want Mexican, just say so."

We started talking about what we felt like eating. Finally I noticed that Isabelle wasn't joining in.

"Is something wrong?" I asked. "Don't you want to get something to eat?"

"It isn't that," said Isabelle, looking troubled. "It's just—look, you've all been so nice these past two weeks. But I sort of feel like I'm butting in on a private party."

My friends got quiet.

"I'll tell you what," said Isabelle. "You five go off and do whatever you usually do when you come here. I'll meet you at France right before the performance. No one will ever know that we split up. Okay?"

I felt terrible. I had been trying to include Isabelle as much as possible. But I hadn't even thought about what she might be feeling.

"I'm sorry," said Paula. "We didn't mean to—"

"I've got an idea," I interrupted her. "I'll hang out with Isabelle. You guys go to Mexico. And we'll all sit together at the performance."

The other Disney Girls didn't look thrilled with this idea, but what could they do? After giving me some meaningful looks, they left. Isabelle and I wandered down to Morocco. I just love Morocco. I feel so comfortable there. It has a special alcove with a bench and a small fountain on the wall. Behind the fountain is a mirror. For some reason it makes me feel refreshed and calm.

"I'm sorry," Isabelle said miserably, after we had sat down. "This is all my fault. If I hadn't horned in on you and your friends—"

"Don't be silly," I said briskly. "I asked you to be my field-trip buddy, remember?"

"Oh, you were just being nice," Isabelle sighed. "The problem is, I'm a total oddball. Remember how I said I didn't really fit in at my old school?"

I nodded.

Isabelle hung her head. "The truth is, I don't really fit in *anywhere*."

It suddenly seemed like the perfect time for me to test my secret theory. "That's not true," I told her, "because you fit in with me. With all of us."

"What do you mean?" Isabelle asked.

I took a deep breath. "Look." I turned her head to face the mirror in back of the fountain. A thin, sparkling stream of water trickled down in front of it, making music like bells as it hit the tiles below.

"Look," I repeated. We both gazed deeply into the mirror. Under my breath, I murmured,

> "All the magic powers that be,
> Hear me now, my special plea.
> Of worldly sights please set us free,
> And help us see what we should be."

Slowly the air around us blurred and faded as we stared at ourselves in the mirror. Right before our eyes, my hair grew darker, my eyes turned brown . . . and I became Jasmine. I heard Isabelle gasp. But she was changing, too. In a few moments, she changed from being a pretty African American girl into being Belle, with long brown hair in a ponytail and brown eyes.

"See?" I whispered.

"I do see," Isabelle whispered back. "And—I have something to tell you."

I held my breath as our images faded from the mirror. Soon we just looked like our usual selves again. I blinked.

The sun was still shining and we were still at EPCOT. But for a few moments, we had definitely been somewhere else.

"I've never told anyone this," continued Isabelle. "But when I saw *Beauty and the Beast*—it was like it wasn't even a movie. It was the story of my life, even though we look so different."

"I know," I said, nodding.

"It was as if everything Belle thought or said or did—"

"You could say or think or do," I finished for her. "It was as if you really *were* Belle. Like you were one person."

She looked at me, wide-eyed. "Yes, that's right. And you're . . . Jasmine?"

I grinned. "Yep. I'm just like you. And so are Ella, Paula, Ariel, Yukiko. We're the Disney Girls. And now I know you're one, too."

# Chapter Fourteen

# Talk About Magic

For the next ten minutes, Isabelle and I talked so much, so fast, that I don't think anyone could have understood us. But it all came out: how eerie it had been for her, seeing the movie. How sometimes she looked in a mirror and saw Belle looking out—just as we had a few minutes before.

And I told her all about me, and how lucky I had been to meet Yukiko in ballet class.

"Even though I'm blond and have green eyes, still, I just *am* Jasmine inside. I feel it," I told her.

Isabelle nodded. "I know exactly what you mean."

The minutes disappeared, and all of a sudden it was time to race over to France and meet everyone for the dance performance.

We waited in front of the pavilion, and soon saw Ella, Yukiko, Ariel, and Paula run up, breathless.

"She's a Disney Girl!" I practically shrieked as soon as they were close enough. I made sure no one else could hear us, and then I quickly explained who Isabelle really was.

"No," said Paula in amazement, staring at Isabelle. "You're kidding. There can't be *six* of us."

"There are," I said. "Really and truly."

The others listened as I told them about seeing her in the mirror, and Isabelle confirmed it.

"Do you have a special charm?" Ariel asked.

Isabelle nodded. "I have a tiny silver mirror that I wear on a chain. My father gave it to me. Do you all have charms, too?"

"Yep," I said. "Mine is a gold lamp. I wear it either as a bracelet or a necklace."

"I have a little heart locket," said Yukiko.

Isabelle frowned, thinking and gazing at her. Then she

smiled. "Snow White. The heart is for the heart that the stepmother told the hunter to bring back."

"That's right," said Yukiko, pleased.

"I have a seashell charm," said Ariel.

"You're easy," laughed Isabelle. "Anyone who knows you for five minutes can tell you're Ariel."

"My charm is a crystal slipper," said Ella.

"Cinderella," said Isabelle promptly. She looked into Ella's eyes. "Yes, I can see it."

"This is mine," said Paula. She pulled her necklace out from beneath her T-shirt. It was a silver chain strung with small turquoise beads. The charm hanging from it was a silver feather.

"Pocahontas," said Isabelle thoughtfully. "Of course."

She stepped back and looked at the five us. "I see it now," she said wonderingly. "I see who you are. I don't know why I didn't see it before."

"Sometimes the real world gets in the way," I said, and everyone laughed and nodded.

"There you are, girls," said Mr. Murchison, behind us. "Come inside quickly and sit down. The performance is about to begin."

So the six of us raced into the pavilion and found our seats. We sat down just as the lights dimmed and the music began. Then we were transported into a beautiful world of international dance.

I loved the performance, but I could hardly pay attention to it. Inside, my mind was swirling with happiness. I couldn't believe it. Once again, magic had worked in my life. I knew Ella, Ariel, Paula, Yukiko, and I would all be closer than ever. But the most wonderful thing of all was that I finally had a real, live, *best* best friend of my very own. Who knew what adventures we would have this coming year? When you have magic in your life, anything can happen. But one thing I knew for sure: together, the six of us would always be . . . the Disney Girls.

# Disney Girls

## #2 Attack of the Beast

Now I was really steaming. My parents and the McIlhennys had lived next door to each other since before Kenny and I were born. Mr. McIlhenny and my dad work at the same company. Kenny had been a rock in my shoe for as long as I could remember. He had thrown sand at me when we were toddlers. He had pretended to eat a frog and made me cry when we were in kindergarten. He had thrown water balloons at me every summer, my whole life. He had leaped out of bushes at me, made prank phone calls, and wrote "Isabelle is a total sissy" on our wooden fence with chalk. Throughout everything, I had tried to ignore him, tried to rise above his stupid childishness, tried to handle it so I wouldn't upset my parents.

But now he had gone too far.

"Guys," I said grimly. "The Beast spied on us. He's ruined our sleepover. And he probably videotaped us doing private Disney Girls stuff. I think you all know what this means."

One by one I met my friends' eyes. Ella and Yukiko seemed timid and a little fearful. Paula was curious. Ariel had a look of outrage on her face. Jasmine waited for me to finish.

"This means war," I said.

# Read all of the books in the
## Disney Girls series!

### #1 One of Us

Jasmine is thrilled to be a Disney Girl. It means she has four best friends—Ariel, Yukiko, Paula, and Ella. But she still doesn't have a *best* best friend. Then she meets Isabelle Beaumont, the new girl. Maybe Isabelle could be Jasmine's best best friend— but could she be a *Disney Girl*?

### #2 Attack of the Beast

Isabelle's next-door neighbor Kenny has been a total Beast for as long as she can remember. But now he's gone too far: he secretly videotaped the Disney Girls singing and dancing and acting silly at Isabelle's slumber party. Isabelle vows to get the tape back, but how will she ever get past the Beast?

### #3 And Sleepy Makes Seven

Mrs. Hayashi is expecting a baby soon, and Yukiko is praying that this time it'll be a girl. She's already got six younger brothers and stepbrothers, and this is her last chance for a sister. All of the Disney Girls are hoping that with a little magic, Yukiko's fondest wish will come true.

### #4 A Fish out of Water

Ariel in ballet class? That's like putting a fish in the middle of the desert! Even though Ariel's the star of her swim team, she decides that she wants to spend more time with the other Disney Girls. So she joins Jasmine and Yukiko's ballet class. But has Ariel made a mistake, or will she trade in her flippers for toe shoes forever?

### #5  *Cinderella's Castle*

The Disney Girls are so excited about the school's holiday party. Ella decides that the perfect thing for her to make is an elaborate gingerbread castle. But creating such a complicated confection isn't easy, even for someone as superorganized as Ella. And her stepfamily just doesn't seem to understand how important this is to her. Ella could really use a fairy godmother right now. . . .

### #6  *One Pet Too Many*

Paula's always loved animals, any animal. Who else would have a pet raccoon, not to mention two cats, a dog, three rabbits, and countless fish? When Paula finds a lost baby armadillo, though, her parents say, "No more pets!"—and that's that. But how much trouble could a baby armadillo be? Plenty, as Paula discovers—especially when she's trying to keep it a secret from her parents.

### #7  *Adventure in Walt Disney World:*
### *A Disney Girls Super Special*

The Disney Girls are so excited. They're all going to dress up as their favorite Disney Princesses and participate in the Magic Kingdom Princess Parade. And as a special treat, Jasmine's mom is taking them to stay overnight at a hotel in the park. Magical things are bound to happen to the Disney Girls in the most magical place on earth—and they do. . . .